For Jamie and Henry

Other titles in the Alfie series:

Alfie's Feet

Alfie Gives a Hand

An Evening at Alfie's

Alfie and the Birthday Surprise

Alfie Wins a Prize

Alfie and the Big Boys

Alfie Weather

Alfie's World

Annie Rose is my Little Sister

Rhymes for Annie Rose

The Big Alfie and Annie Rose Storybook

The Big Alfie Out of Doors Storybook

ALFIE GETS IN FIRST
A RED FOX BOOK 978 1 862 30783 4

First published in Great Britain by The Bodley Head, an imprint of Random House Children's Publishers UK
A Random House Group Company

The Bodley Head edition published 1981
Red Fox first edition published 1991
This Red Fox edition published 2009

9 10 8

Copyright © Shirley Hughes, 1981

The right of Shirley Hughes to be identified as the author and illustrator of this work has been asserted in accordance
with the Copyright, Designs and Patents Act 1988.

Red Fox Books are published by Random House Children's Publishers UK, 61–63 Uxbridge Road, London W5 5SA

www.randomhousechildrens.co.uk
www.alfiebooks.co.uk

Addresses for companies within The Random House Group Limited can be found at: www.randomhouse.co.uk/offices.htm

THE RANDOM HOUSE GROUP Limited Reg. No. 954009

A CIP catalogue record for this book is available from the British Library.

The Random House Group Limited supports The Forest Stewardship Council® (FSC),the leading international forest-certification organization.
Our books carrying the FSC label are printed on FSC®-certified paper. FSC is the only forest-certification scheme supported by the leading
environmental organizations, including Greenpeace. Our paper procurement policy can be found at www.randomhouse.co.uk/environment

Printed in Italy

ALFIE

Alfie Gets in First

Shirley Hughes

Red Fox

One day Alfie and Mum and Annie Rose were coming home from the shops. Alfie ran on ahead because he wanted to get home first. He ran all the way from the corner to the front gate and up the steps to the front door.

Then he sat down on the top step and
waited for the others. Along came Mum,
pushing Annie Rose and the shopping.

"I raced you!" called Alfie. "I'm back
first, so there!"

Annie Rose didn't care. She was tired.
She sat back in her push-chair and sucked
her thumb.

Mum put the brake on the push-chair and
left Annie Rose at the bottom of the steps
while she lifted the basket of shopping up to
the top. Then she found the key and opened
the front door. Alfie dashed in ahead of her.

"I've won, I've won!" he shouted.

Mum put the shopping down in the hall and went
back down the steps to lift Annie Rose out of her
push-chair. But what do you think Alfie did then?

He gave the door a great big slam – BANG!
– just like that.

Then Mum was outside the door, holding
Annie Rose, and Alfie was inside with the
shopping. Mum's key was inside too.

"Open the door, Alfie," said Mum.

But Alfie didn't know how to open the door from the inside. The catch was too high up. Mum looked into the letter-box.

"Try to reach the catch and turn it," she said. Alfie tried but he couldn't quite reach it.

"Can you put the key through the letter-box?" said Mum. But Alfie couldn't reach the letter-box either.

Annie Rose was hungry as well as tired. She began to cry. Then Alfie began to cry too. He didn't like being all by himself on the wrong side of the door. Just then Mrs MacNally came hurrying across the street to see what all the noise was about.

She and Mum took it in turns to say
encouraging things into the letter-box.
But Alfie still couldn't open the door.

"Go and fetch your little chair from the sitting-room and then you'll be able to reach the catch," said Mum. But Alfie didn't try to fetch his little chair. He just went on crying, louder and louder, and Annie Rose cried louder and louder too.

"There's my Maureen," said Mrs MacNally. "I'm sure she'll be able to help."

Mrs MacNally's Maureen was a big girl. Right away she came and joined Mum and Annie Rose and Mrs MacNally on the top step.

"Mmm, might have to break a window," she said. "But I'll try to climb up the drain-pipe first, if you like."

But Mrs MacNally didn't like that idea at all.

"Oh no, Maureen, you might hurt yourself," she said.

Just then Alfie's very good friend the milkman came up the street in his milk-float.

When he saw Mum and Annie Rose and Mrs MacNally
and Mrs MacNally's Maureen all standing on the top
step he stopped his float and said:

"What's the trouble?"

So they told him.

"Don't worry, mate," the milkman shouted. "We'll
soon have you out of there."

"Mmm, looks as though this lock's going to be difficult to break," said the milkman. But then Mrs MacNally's Maureen had a very good idea. She ran to ask the window-cleaner, who was working up the street, if he would bring his ladder and climb up to the bathroom window. And, of course, when the window-cleaner heard about Alfie he came hurrying along with his ladder as quickly as he could.

Then Mum and Annie Rose and Mrs MacNally and Mrs MacNally's Maureen and the milkman all stood on the top step and watched while the window-cleaner put his ladder up against the house. He started to climb up to the bathroom window. But when he was half-way up the ladder, what do you think happened?

The front door suddenly opened and there was Alfie! He had managed to reach the catch and turn it – like that – after all.

He was *very* pleased with himself. He opened the front door as wide as it would go and stood back grandly to let everybody in.

Then the window-cleaner came down from his
ladder, and he and the milkman and Mrs MacNally's
Maureen and Mrs MacNally and Annie Rose and Mum
and Alfie all went into the kitchen and had tea together.